25 MINUTES

FOR YOU ARE A MIST THAT APPEARS FOR A LITTLE TIME AND THEN VANISHES.

CHIRADEEP PATRA

A writer has no worth without a reader who reads and motivates them to write more. So, I dedicate this book to all my readers, those who love to read and support what I write by weaving the words of my imagination.

I also dedicate this book to those who have inspired me all these years and have prompted me to write such stories.

ᐅᐅᐅ

Contents

Foreword   *vii*

Preface   *ix*

Acknowledgements   *xi*

  1. It's Time   1

  2. Chicken Hearted Donkey   3

  3. Surgery Is Over   7

Epilogue   11

Foreword

Being friends with Chiradeep is like being friends with the dawn—the warmth after the dark chill of the night, the sense of wonderment at the beauty of this world bathed in the golden glow of the rising sun, and above all, the hope of a new beginning. Chiradeep is all that and much more, and so are his writings.

I first met him in 2016 when I was only a blogger, trying to find my feet in the writing world. I'm still lame, hobbling on one leg, but Chiradeep, or Dada—the universal big brother—as he's called by everyone who knows him, has been with me all along the way. From talking an eternal pessimist into writing positive articles on holistic health and wellness for his magazine–*Candles Online*, to discussing my writing process and problems, to cheering me on even when he was, and still is, suffering from bouts of bad health, he has been my champion. I may not expect my family to support my struggle in writing and may not expect my friends to appreciate what I do, but I know Dada is always a phone call away to cheer me on, and he will be the first to drop in a comment of praise, even if it's undeserved. For he loves unconditionally, and his love knows no bounds.

Coming to the writing part of this multi-faceted man, his articles have the singular purpose of helping humanity. From religion to work-related issues, he has, in a career spanning 16 years, written, to my knowledge, on every aspect of health and well-being. He started Candles as a charitable publication in 2006 and became an e-magazine in 2015. Throughout that period, he managed it on his own while handling a job as an accountant. But the most significant task was exhorting his contributors (like me) to write articles for the magazine. He was an affable dictator when it came to that. He wouldn't back down even if you said no for the hundredth time. But this dogged approach endears him to his Candles family, readers and anyone acquainted with him.

I've been associated with this talented, generous and patient soul for many years now, and I can vouch that what he writes comes from a deep well of experience, pain and cherished happiness found in the small mercies of life. If Chiradeep Patra writes on a topic, it's a given. It has been written in words measured with care and love so that nothing but pure positivity is conveyed to the reader. Believe me, he's the agent of God, and he wants nothing but the best for the world. If a family is a little world created with love, Dada's world rivals the very Earth.

The story is swift and to the point; the end is poignant yet satisfying and leaves the reader with a profound message of believing in silver linings in the darkest clouds. True to his nature, Dada imbues the story with bittersweet moments, like itself, because this story is not fiction at all, even if the characters be fictitious. This story could be yours or mine or the neighbour's, which makes it so relatable. I am glad to have had the chance to read it first, and I'm even happier that I am the one who gets to introduce it to you. Be prepared to feel the warm light of the dawn of new beginnings, dear readers, and enjoy the book.

Pradita Kapahi
Writer & Blogger

Preface

It gives me great joy in introducing this thoughtful and very emotional short story to you readers. On February 20th 2001, I met a girl lying on the stretcher as I was on another, about to go for my second heart surgery in the Manipal Heart Foundation, Bengaluru. We just smiled, looking at each other, realising we both were going for the same procedure. Using this little fact of my life, I construed an utterly fictional story for my readers to wonder about and be inspired. Why should I be telling anything more about the story before you read it?

I don't want to be a spoiler. Enjoy!!!

♡♡♡

Acknowledgements

My heart is ever so grateful to God for giving me the idea and strength to write this book, the first storybook I am publishing. Therefore, I humbly acknowledge God, who helped me to write this story to stir the emotions in the hearts and minds of the readers.

My all-time inspiration has been my uncle, Samuel Patro. He is a storyteller, and I am privileged to have gained a knack for storytelling like him. I am grateful to him for inspiring me so much.

I am grateful to the dynamic Pradita Kapahi, the rockstar Sis, as I call her, for writing a foreword for this book and endorsing me as a writer. She is a fantastic writer with feathers of legal expertise in her kitty who has inspired me a lot in writing quality and well-presented stories. I sincerely acknowledge the contribution of her ideas and suggestions for the improvement of this book.

The word queen, Saakshi Gupta, has always been very supportive throughout these years of my writing - editing my works on the blog space we commonly share. She is an excellent writer who can write in any genre. I am thankful to her for extending her precious help towards this book, from proofreading to editing it wonderfully. I am indebted to Saak for her invaluable efforts and input in publishing this storybook.

Ultimately, I thank all my family members and friends far and wide who have always supported me to venture ahead to publish this book.

❦❦❦

ONE

IT'S TIME

It was 4:30 AM. Sarah woke him up. "*Suraj, get up. You need to take a bath.*"

"*Now?*" He was surprised as well as scared. He knows when a goat is taken for slaughter, it is fed and given a bath.

He didn't have a choice. He followed her instructions word by word.

At around 7 AM, his parents visited him and tried to give him courage, though they were panicky for their only son. His mother's eyes were moist, his father sported a wry smile, and Suraj looked pale.

"*It's time.*" Sarah reappeared, and his parents stood aside. She pulled along a wheelchair and requested Suraj to sit on it. He protested as he could have walked. But the nurse made him understand the hospital protocol. They must follow it. He obliged and bade goodbye to his parents as Sarah pulled the wheelchair to the elevator.

The scenario of a typical hospital ward and an ICCU or Operation Theatre is entirely different. The regular hospital wards have more patients and less of nurses, doctors and hospital staff. But in an ICCU or OT, there are several doctors and nurses for a few negligible numbers of patients.

And the rushing of nurses and doctors was all the scarier to watch.

Suraj's heart was pounding like crazy in his chest, ready to burst and leap out of his diaphragm and ribcage, leaving him alone. Sarah asked him to get off the wheelchair, and another nurse instructed him to lie on a stretcher. He did so and was looking at Sarah, as she was the only one giving him a modicum of strength at that moment.

She cradled his hand and assured him, "*Nothing will happen; see you soon. God will be with you.*" And the gurney wheels rolled as Sarah was left behind while the other nurse towed it into another room.

"*Stay calm and wait here; I will take you in when the time of surgery comes.*" She said and left Suraj alone in that sterile room wrought with the smell of iodine, antiseptic, and fear.

ϸϸϸ

TWO

CHICKEN HEARTED DONKEY

After a couple of minutes, another stretcher was pulled into the room. It wasn't an empty one, but a girl was lying on it. The nurse pulled that stretcher beside him and left. He saw the clock hanging on the wall of that room. It was precisely 7:35 AM.

She looked at Suraj, and he looked back at her. They didn't take even a single nanosecond to hold back their smiles, as they could relate to each other very well in that condition in the hospital.

"Hey", She whispered with a lovely smile on her beautiful face. She had sharp features, a long nose, vivid eyes, and succulent pink lips. But she was lean and thin like him. Suraj observed.

"You are also waiting for surgery?" She asked again, bringing Suraj back to his senses as he was lost in her beauty.

"Yeah, yeah. I am waiting for it. You too?" He asked her back, to which she nodded.

"I am Shekinah. You?" She was prompt and very cheerful.

"I am Suraj." He replied with a pleasant smile.

"You are a CHD, Suraj?" She asked again.

"Yes, I am. How about you?" He posed the same question.

She nodded and asked, *"Do you know the full form of CHD?"*

"Yes, Coronary Heart Disease," Suraj replied quickly.

"Nah," she giggled mischievously, turning side-wise on the stretcher she was lying on.

Suraj also turned on his side, facing her. *"What is it, then?"* he asked incredulously.

"Chicken Hearted Donkey, that's what you are...." She chuckled.

"Seriously? Why? How?" Suraj was taken aback by her free-spirited attitude.

"We are in the same condition. Look at me; I am so joyful. And look at you, scared, thus chicken-hearted." She kept giggling.

"Ah, okay. I agree. But why Donkey?" Suraj was amused by her explanation and enquired further.

"D for Donkey. Nothing else comes to my mind. It can also be a dog, but I can't call you one. So, Donkey it is." She stated as they both burst into laughter.

"You are something, Shekinah. Wow, C-H-D." After a slight pause, Suraj kept repeating the words; he remarked, *"By the way, Shekinah, you don't seem to be a CHD at all."*

"Hmm, maybe. Yet, here I am. See, I am waiting for my surgery." She scoffed.

"But I didn't mean that, CHD. I meant your version of CHD, which you are not." He said with a naughty grin.

"*Wow, someone's singing my song. Nice.*" Shekinah laughed as if she had achieved something.

Suraj couldn't believe that he was already feeling slightly better and lighter since Shekinah's arrival in that dreadful room. He wondered how this girl could cut such jokes at this time of the hour in her life and even lift the spirit of another. Her beautiful sparkling eyes, her smiles... 'Ah, he is getting sucked into her charm and aura,' He thought.

"*But...*" She sighed after a moment, "*it was discovered much later, at 20. I am 21 now. I wish it would have been discovered much earlier.*" She seemed serious.

"*Anyway, here I am for surgery; I am hopeful I will jump around again and have fun. May not be like others, but like us.*" She chuckled again.

'US', the word stirred something inside Suraj. A sense of belonging.

"*When do you get to know that you are a CHD?*" she prompted him.

Suraj had no intention of uttering even a word. All he wanted to do was watch her cheerful demeanour and dazzling smile and listen to her speak as her words flow like a crystal-clear stream.

"*Hey, Suraj. Don't tell me you lost your senses in my presence.*" She quipped.

"*Gosh, NO!.*" He blushed and could not hide it from her. She seemed to enjoy it thoroughly.

"*I have been a CHD, 'your version' all this time. But I think I will change that after this surgery. What do you think?*" He added and sought her opinion.

"*Looks like I have influenced you a lot. Not bad.*" She teased.

"*How do you remain calm and cheerful even before such a major surgery?*" He was curious.

"*How can I help myself by worrying? Stressing about it won't help me; it just piles on my problems. Moreover, God is in control, He knows what's best for me, for all of us.*" She acknowledged the matter.

"*Hmm. I got your point. But… you are commendable, honestly.*" He couldn't resist expressing it.

"*Suraj? Are you going to propose to me now?*" She laughed.

Suraj sat up on the stretcher, and it rolled a bit with his sudden movement.

"*Careful, man. You will fall off the stretcher; I was talking about falling for me.*" She continued as she lifted her head, resting on her elbow.

"*You are too much, Shekinah. But I seriously enjoyed you so much.*" Suraj said as he lay on his belly.

"*You haven't enjoyed me yet, Suraj.*" She laughed and added, "*But I wanted you to enjoy me in the future if you are still up for it. Should we meet up after we come out of this place?*" Her tone carried hints of mischief and adventure.

"*Sure.*" Suraj was ecstatic.

And they both promised to meet up after their surgery. It was sharp at 8 AM when Suraj was pulled out of the room on the stretcher. Shekinah smiled, looked at him, and gave him a thumbs up. Suraj waved his hand. He was already missing Shekinah.

ϷϷϷ

THREE

SURGERY IS OVER

Two days passed in the ICCU, and he was in utter pain from the fresh wound he had because of the surgery. The nurses in the ICCU were extremely busy and focused on the critical patients, and Suraj couldn't get anyone's attention. After the waste blood was drained out of his body and the pipe was removed from his chest, he was taken back to the ward he was in before surgery.

As soon as he was shifted to the ward, he looked for Sarah, but it wasn't her shift then.

Someone else was there in the ward. He politely asked her to collect information about Shekinah, who got operated on the same day of his surgery. She nodded, but she never inquired about her. Suraj was disappointed as his heart and mind were seeking information about Shekinah.

The following day, when Suraj woke up, he saw Sarah in the ward. She smiled and came to him.

"Congratulation, Suraj. I am so happy to see you back." She shook his hand.

"Thank you, sister Sarah. I want a favour from you, please." He was in no mood for unnecessary pleasantries with her at that moment.

"*What is it, Suraj?*" Sarah enquired curiously.

"*Please, enquire about a patient named Shekinah on the fourth floor operated on the same day. Please do it for me.*" He pleaded with Sarah.

Sarah and Suraj had already established a friendship apart from this patient and nurse relationship, and she immediately inquired about Shekinah on the fourth floor.

Sarah returned after 10-15 minutes and stood by Suraj's bed.

"*Tell me, could you gather any whereabouts of her?*" Suraj's heartbeats were racing.

"*Yes. Her operation was successful as yours, and she is doing fine.*" Sarah said, clutching her fingers around his as she could see the joy spreading through his face.

"*Happy?*" she asked.

He blushed and said, "*Yes, I am delighted. You know Sarah; she is so gorgeous.*"

"*Really?*" She smirked and was thrilled to see her patient friend was so happy.

Every day when she used to do her shift in that ward, Suraj would talk about Shekinah and his feelings for her. And every day, Sarah would enquire about Shekinah and inform Suraj she was recovering faster than he was.

He was discharged from the hospital nine days after his surgery. His parents came to take him with them. Sarah was there, and he asked her to do the last favour before he left the hospital.

"*Please help me visit the fourth floor to see Shekinah before I leave.*" He requested.

"*Oh shoot. I forgot to tell you.*" Sarah replied instantly.

"*What?*" He looked at her eagerly.

"*She was discharged this morning. I had enquired earlier.*" She said.

"That's not possible. She promised me she would meet up before leaving, and I promised the same to her." He felt sad.

Sarah tried to make him understand like a good friend, but that news aggrieved Suraj. *"Oh, come on, buddy. Don't take it to heart. She must have said it just to cheer you up. If you are destined to meet her, God will let you meet her again. Now, stop thinking about her and go back home and call me on my cell number."* Sarah comforted him while he was leaving.

Suraj was home. He had a lot of post-surgery restrictions, which he needed to follow religiously. His relatives kept visiting their house to see him.

Days passed by, but Shekinah was still in his heart and mind. He was in utter disbelief that she could go away before meeting him. He would always discuss her when he called up Sarah. And she would patiently listen to him as a good friend.

One day, Sarah finally revealed the truth to Suraj. *"Shekinah had succumbed on the OT table that day itself, Suraj. I couldn't have shared that dreadful news when you were so weak and recovering. So, I kept that thorn in my heart this long, waiting for you to be strong enough to digest this about the one you had fallen for."*

Suraj could not speak for the next few minutes as he hung up the phone. Shekinah's image flashed in front of him. She gave her strength but succumbed to the deadly foe of life. The one who taught him to stay jovial in the face of trouble was the prey to it. Suraj felt as if he had lost a vital organ of his body. Those 25 minutes he spent with her were the most valuable moments he will treasure for the rest of his life.

Years later, Suraj was standing in front of a crowd of young people, inspiring them on how to deal with life's challenges by carrying out our responsibilities as human beings. While delivering his speech, he made sure to highlight Shekinah and her contribution to his life. He understood that even though our lives are just a mist that emerges for a short while before dissipating, we may still be valuable to others.

ᐩᐩᐩ

Epilogue

"Now listen, you who say, "Today or tomorrow we will go to this or that city, spend a year there, carry on business and make money." Why, you do not even know what will happen tomorrow. What is your life? **You are a mist that appears for a little while and then vanishes**. *Instead, you ought to say, "If it is the Lord's will, we will live and do this or that." As it is, you boast in your arrogant schemes. All such boasting is evil. If anyone, then, knows the good they ought to do and doesn't do it, it is sin for them."*

Life is a gift from God, and we live it by His grace. God has created us from dust, and we return to dust when life ends. What remains is our spirit; the body rots in the dust. Despite this knowledge, we humans always plan extensively, schedule and reschedule many things for the rat race of life.

One set of people live with this mindset. They have all the worries in this world. But others complain, grumble and lead a life of self-pity and insecurity. And they can't see anything good happening to them.

If we analyse, we will realise that the root cause of both mindsets are PRIDE and BOASTING. Whether we scheme big or do nothing out of self-pity, we do it with arrogance and pride in our hearts.

In the Bible passage cited in the beginning from James 4:13-17, we find an undeniable truth about human life. It is just a mist that appears for a little while before disappearing. Humans need to depend on God's will and

His plans for our lives. Our times are not in our own hands but at God's disposal. Our hearts and minds may be filled with all the care for ourselves, our families, and our friends, but we fail in everything we thought was perfect.

I realised this truth when I underwent my second heart surgery in 2001. Patients of all ages were present, from babies to the elderly. In my experience, I have seen beautiful girls and handsome boys suffer from unimaginable heart conditions. There, I realised God had given me a much better life than many of them who were admitted for treatment.

The protagonist of my story, Ms Shekinah, takes us through a reality check about how fleeting our arrogance, pride, beauty, and strength are. And she, before disappearing as a mist, did a commendable job. She taught Suraj (another character in my story) the true meaning of life. A life without worries and self-pity but dependent on God, the Sustainer.

ppp